C.H.O.M.P.S.*

*Canine HOMe Protection System

C.H.O.M.P.S.*

from the Hanna-Barbera/American International Productions' Film

Book by Vic Crume

Screenplay by Dick Robbins,
Duane Poole and Joseph Barbera

based on a story by Joseph Barbera

*Canine HOMe Protection System

SCHOLASTIC BOOK SERVICES
NEW YORK • TORONTO • LONDON • AUCKLAND • SYDNEY • TOKYO

ISBN 0-590-30528-X

12 11 10 9 8 7 6 5 4 3 2 1   1   0 1 2 3 4 5/8

Printed in the U.S.A.   06

From the TV screen, Hamilton's Chief of Police was thanking everyone in town for inviting him into their living rooms. But few viewers of the evening news broadcast bothered to listen either to Chief Patterson's thanks, or to the dire warnings which followed, about criminal activity in Hamilton.

After all, there never had been a crime wave in this pleasant town, and few residents figured they were rich enough to be stolen from. It was Chief Patterson's thankless task to rouse the indifferent citizenry.

"Not one of you watching me now is safe from the hoodlums who are invading our homes," he said. He leaned toward the cameras. "And don't believe your house is safe *just because you are there*."

Even as he spoke, in one of Hamilton's living rooms, a thick wallet was being deftly transferred from its owner's jacket pocket to a burglar's sack. The owner, blissfully unaware, munched steadily on his TV dinner and waited for the sportscast to begin.

In the house next door, dinner was not quite ready. The head of the house snoozed in his chair before the TV. His wife, at the kitchen door, waved a bunch of celery toward the set. "Paul! You're not even listening! *Please* turn off that noise!"

"Yeah. Sure," her husband answered groggily — and snoozed on.

"They'll steal valuables right out from under your nose," the Chief said forcefully from the screen.

"Paul! *Please* turn that off."

This time, her request got results. A burglar obliged. Disconnecting the set, he quietly lifted it off the stand and handed it over to his pal just outside the window.

"Thank you!" Paul's wife trilled from the kitchen.

By the time the celery was in the salad, the family TV was in a van, moving briskly along the streets of Hamilton.

Another Hamilton resident, bachelor Brian Foster, also had not heard the Chief's broadcast. Yet, as Chief Engineer of Alarms Systems for Norton Industries, he could have written the Chief's message.

For an employee whose alarms systems were doing nothing to lower Hamilton's crime rate, Brian was feeling very cheerful as he steered his aging car into the supermarket parking lot. There was barely time before closing to pick up a quart of milk for himself and a large economy size bag of Doggie Diet Delight for Rascal.

If ever a dog deserved something delightful it was Rascal. "Without Rascal," Brian told the dog pictured on the bag, "I'd never have thought up C.H.O.M.P.S." He moved forward in the check-out lane, still talking. "Rascal! The way you've let me copy you — measure your legs, your nose, your tail... and now Chomps—"

"Beg pardon, sir?" asked the girl at the cash register.

Brian flushed. "I was just saying my dog likes to *chomp* on these things."

Quickly he pocketed his change and hurried out to his car. Parked between two low-slung sportscars, it looked even older than it was—not the kind of car a rising young executive would choose to own. But every spare cent Brian made in the last three years had gone into perfecting Chomps. "Oh, well," he sighed as he slid behind the wheel, "someday I'll have a real car. Have a wife, too. Heck! I'll be so rich I'll even turn on *two* lights—with the TV going at the same time!"

Brian's monthly electricity bill was real cause for alarm. Now he worried, "Did I, or did I not leave the TV going when I left the house? I know I put Chomps on 'housedog,' but —oh, well—" He drove into the street.

At almost that moment, a prowler stepped from the shadows of Brian's patio and moved up to a window. All he could see, in the darkening room, was Chief Patterson on the TV screen. Swiftly, the prowler moved to the patio door, unaware that at least two ears were tuned in on the Chief's speech.

"What steps can we take," asked the Chief, "to combat this assault on our privacy?"

There was a first faint sound of a lock-pick at the front door. Two raggedy ears perked up. Two eyes began to glow with a reddish light. CLICK. The lock sprung. And like a small thunderbolt the owner of the glowing eyes shot across the room.

With a tremendous karate kick, a little dog flung himself against the door. Back flew the door against the wall, knocking the prowler flat behind it. On went the raggedy thunderbolt. Then, skidding to a stop, it turned a reddish glare on the intruder.

The would-be burglar lost no time in making a flying dive to the fence. He sailed over it— straight through the open window of a car parked at the curb. Legs still flailing the air, he yelled to his accomplice, "Dig out — and *fast!*"

The car burned rubber just in time. CRASH! A wrenching, splintering sound filled the air. Out from the white board fence came the four-legged fury. Then, almost as fast as the red taillights vanished down the street; the red glowing eyes faded down to normal dog-color.

Up drove Brian. He took in the situation at a glance. "Chomps! All *right*. That was one surprised burglar. You really *work*." Hopping out of the car, he slapped his hand against Chomps' outstretched paw. "It's about time I told the boss about you."

Suddenly he frowned. "But I thought I'd programmed you for 'housedog.' How'd you get on 'watchdog'?" He sighed. "There are still some bugs to work out."

Belatedly, an exact duplicate of Chomps came tail-wagging over from next door where he'd been paying an early evening call on Brian's neighbor, Mrs. Elvira Fowler. Rascal enjoyed Mrs. Fowler's company, but he was really crazy about Muffin, her dainty Pekinese. Possibly it was the ribbon Muffin wore in her hair. At any rate, Muffin had been the ruin of Rascal as a good guard dog.

And so, in a way, Muffin was responsible for the Chief Engineer of Alarms Systems creating Chomps. C.H.O.M.P.S. — Canine Home Protection System, "Chomps" for short.

Now, with Rascal's loving heart and Chomps' strictly-business-all-computer insides, Brian had all anyone could ask of dogdom—love *and* security.

Into the house went the trio. Chomps trotted along between Rascal and Brian. In the kitchen, Brian gave Rascal his dinner, then patting two raggedy heads, strolled out to hear the very last of Chief Patterson's alarming talk.

2

Bright sunshine beaming into the spacious office of R. J. Norton, President of Norton Industries, did nothing to brighten R.J.'s gloomy face. He looked up as Ken Sharp, his second-in-command, entered.

"Where's Foster?" he snapped.

"Brian just now called, R.J." Ken Sharp grinned. "He said he'd be a little late."

"*Late!*" R.J. thundered. "Well, where is he?"

"He said something unexpected turned up."

"Something *unexpected*! Sharp, I don't expect anything unexpected to turn up when I call an emergency meeting."

Nervously, R.J. swung his chair toward the

TV set. "We might as well catch the morning newscast while we're waiting." He flipped the remote control button.

Unfortunately, the morning news at that moment featured Chief Patterson's talk from the night before. "This crime situation is intolerable," said the chief.

"Intolerable!" roared R.J. "It's an *emergency*. We're being flooded with complaints about our security systems. If something isn't done soon, Norton Industries will be left with one big, old-fashioned padlock—on *our* front door! We'll be bankrupt!"

Chief Patterson went on in spite of R.J.'s interruption. "Make sure you have *good* locks and security systems. In addition, you might also consider getting a watchdog. *Any* dog that will bark and alert you or your neighbors will make a good watchdog."

R.J. exploded. "A *watchdog*. That's all we need! The business is *already* going to the dogs!"

At the Foster residence Brian had no time for TV viewing. In fact, after Ken Sharp's message to get in to the office for an emergency meeting, Brian hardly had time even for instant coffee. But now, with Chomps safely on zero in the dog carrier, TV turned off, and Rascal watching his frantic master with calm interest, Brian was at least ready to rush out to the driveway.

Rascal, using his private doggie door, trotted out and followed at Brian's heels, then waited for a last good-bye.

"And I want you to stay around the house today, Rascal," said Brian, waving an arm out the car window. "Can't be too careful these days. STAY! Got it?"

Rascal sat down in his best stay-at-home, relaxed manner.

"Good boy!" Brian waved a confident farewell and backed out to the street.

Rascal had the decency to remain seated until the convertible was out of sight. Then, trotting to the edge of the driveway, he carefully double-checked for the all-clear. Right! Brian was definitely vanishing from view. Jauntily, Rascal started out in the opposite direction, looking forward to the day's adventures.

The first interesting possibility was the house at the end of the block. Rascal could usually count on adventure in Monster's backyard — and today he wasn't disappointed. A sign above a large doghouse spelled out MONSTER in capital letters. Rascal could tell, by the large meat bone near the entrance, that the rightful owner must be taking his ease elsewhere, leaving the delicious feast unguarded.

A quick side-to-side check indicated that the heist could be pulled off neatly with no one the wiser. Rascal briskly trotted up to the giant-sized tidbit. Balancing it teeter-totter style, he pranced off. The between-meal snack would be delicious today.

But he hadn't counted on Monster's awakening from a nap behind a large potted fern on the terrace. With a roar Monster was off and running.

Short legs moving like pistons, jaws clamped tight on the bone, Rascal raced for home, with Monster gaining ground in every galloping stride.

Just at this tense moment, a shiny sports car pulled to a stop in Brian's driveway. Out stepped Casey Norton, R.J.'s beautiful daughter and Brian's beautiful fiancée. "Oh, Rascal! Not again!" she cried out.

Rascal shot past her and scooted through the doggie door, the stolen bone barely making it inside with him. Monster, close behind, shot his huge muzzle as far forward as space would allow.

Safe from the great jaws, Rascal, just inches away, calmly sampled his neighbor's property. And as though that was not enough for one huge dog to bear, Monster suddenly felt Casey's hands dragging him away. "Stop that, Monster!" she exclaimed firmly. "*Stop* that. Go on home now. Find someone your own size to pick on."

Monster stared up, twitched his ears in astonishment. Then, lowering his massive head, he started back down the driveway, rumbling a warning to Rascal about what would happen *next* time.

Seeing the coast clear, Rascal pranced out to greet his old friend Casey with a happy bark. She hugged him warmly. "How's it going, Rascal? You just can't seem to stay out of trouble, can you? Now where's Brian?"

"You just missed him, dear," Mrs. Elvira Fowler called from her porch. Cradling the be-ribboned Peke in her arms, she stepped down and gently placed Muffin on the grass. "He drove off about five minutes ago."

"Oh, no!" Casey cried out. "I was hoping to

catch him before he left for my father's office." She stepped toward her car.

"On *Sunday*? My goodness. Your father must be upset about something. Not Brian, I hope?"

"Not upset," Casey called back. "Furious! Maybe I can catch him at the plant. Thank you, Mrs. Fowler." She waved good-bye.

"Not at all," Mrs. Fowler replied and watched Casey speed off. "Isn't she a lovely girl, Muffin? Muffin! Where are you? Oh, dear! She's run off again."

Reaching into her apron pocket she took out a dog whistle and blew on it. Muffin's ears caught the high-pitched note and she came waddling into view. Mrs. Fowler scooped her up. "Now, Muffin," she scolded gently. "How many times must I tell you? You mustn't disappear like that."

Rascal's Monster's, and Mrs. Fowler's problems were nothing compared to the problem Brian was facing in R. J. Norton's office.

He came dashing in, breathless. "I'm sorry I'm late, Mr. Norton." He flung himself down in one of the two matching chairs flanking R.J.'s desk and nodded to Ken.

"I'm sorry, too, Foster," his boss said angrily. "Sorry I ever hired you as my security systems engineer!"

Brian was stunned. Of all the emergencies he'd been thinking of on the way to the meeting, his own job hadn't been one of them.

Ken Sharp seemed to be coming to his rescue. "Mr. Norton," he said smoothly, "you're upset."

"You *bet* I'm upset!" the boss exclaimed. "We're losing customers right and left."

"But, R.J.," Ken Sharp said pleadingly, "when you hired Brian *right out of college*, no experience, you said he was at the top of his class. You hired him because he's brilliant... a genius."

Brian shot a surprised look of gratitude at this unexpected help. He hadn't suspected Ken Sharp of holding this high opinion. In fact, he'd been pretty sure Ken thought Casey Norton should become Mrs. Kenneth Sharp instead of Mrs. Brian Foster.

But R.J. seemed to grow even angrier at Ken's kind words. "If he's so *brilliant*," he sneered, "how come his new security system is such a miserable flop?"

Brian leaned forward. "Mr. Norton," he

began earnestly, "That system is fail-safe. There's no way anyone can penetrate it—unless someone is revealing the secret of its operation."

"He's right, R.J.," said Ken. "That's why you put it right here in your own office." He reached for a pushbutton on Norton's desk. "Why, with that one switch activated, *no* one could get into the office without setting off every alarm in this building." With those words he brought his hand down on the pushbutton.

As though on signal the office door flung open. "Don't move, anybody," a tough voice crunched out.

3

R.J., Ken, and Brian leaped from their chairs in spite of this command. In the doorway, pushing Casey in front of them, were two masked men. One was tall and skinny and the other short and fat, but the ski masks made both equally ferocious-looking.

"Casey!!!" yelled Brian and R.J. together.

Only Ken Sharp kept his mind on Norton Industries. "The alarm! It didn't go off!" he said in a shocked voice.

"Let go of my daughter!" Norton demanded.

"Take it easy, Pops, and she won't get hurt," said Brooks, the thin one.

Brian took one stride forward. "Casey? Are you okay?"

Casey's eyes flashed. "I'm okay. They don't scare me!"

Bracken, the short, fat thief, slapped his hand over Casey's mouth and waved a gun. "She's okay—unless one of you tries to be a hero."

Hero Ken Sharp stepped forward bravely. "Who are you? What do you want? This is an office building! There's nothing you'd want here."

"Yeah? Well—er—" Bracken hesitated.

"How about your wallets? They'll do," Brooks growled. He waved a gun at Bracken, "The bag—quick!"

Promptly the men dropped their wallets into a cloth bag. "Now let go of my daughter!" Norton demanded.

"She follows orders, she doesn't get hurt," said Bracken. "Take off your watches, rings, and empty your pockets."

Casey glared as the three began tugging at rings and sliding off watchbands. "You're not going to *do* it, are you?"

Ken Sharp shrugged helplessly. "What do you say to a man with a gun?"

"How about 'don't shoot,'" Brian murmured.

Brooks kept his eye on his hostage. "Have her put that stuff in the bag."

"Right, Brooks."

"Don't say my name, dummy!"

"Oh! Sure. Sorry, Brooks." He handed the sack to Casey. "Here. Scoop it up in this, sister."

"Don't you 'sister' me," Casey said angrily.

Both burglars waved their guns. "Faster, *sister*!" said Brooks.

"You heard him," Bracken chimed in. "Faster! And put your own rings and stuff in, too."

Angrily, Casey obeyed, then swept the booty on the desk into the sack.

"Okay. Now hand it over."

"You want it in your hand or over the head?" Casey snapped.

Brian paled. "Don't push them, Casey."

"Okay." Brooks nodded. "You've all done great. Don't blow it now and try to call the cops. Open the door, Bracken."

"Don't use my name," Bracken cracked. Keeping a steady eye on the hostages, he fumbled for the doorknob behind the pair.

"Don't nobody move. Got it?" Brooks added. He stared hard at the group as the door behind him swung open. "Okay. Let's go." The two backed through the door slamming it — and shutting themselves in the *closet*!

Like a flash, Brian was across the room. "Call the police," he yelled. "I'll lock them in."

But fast as he was, the ski-masked hoods were faster. Out they tumbled, guns raised. There was no mistaking their deadly mood. "Put down the phone, sis," Brooks ordered.

Casey hesitated.

"I think you'd better do like the man says, Casey," Brian advised.

This time Bracken and Brooks made it to the exit door. "Remember, anyone makes a move and we *waste* you," said Brooks.

Bracken pushed the door. It didn't budge. Aiming his gun, he fired at the doorknob and pushed again. The door held firm.

"Try *pulling* it, dummy," Brooks suggested.

Immediately, the door swung in and Brooks shoved Bracken forward.

For a long moment the robbed foursome stood motionless as the beat of footsteps faded along the hallway. Then R.J. Norton exploded. "That's *it*. That does it." He swung toward Brian. "No wonder we're getting so

18

many complaints about your *brilliant* security system. If those two clowns we just saw can penetrate it—*anybody* can. Foster—you're fired!"

Casey's eyes flared in anger. Ken Sharp shaped his eyebrows into a look of great surprise. And Brian—Brian was nearly speechless. "But, Mr. Norton—"

"No 'buts,' Foster. And no interference, Casey. I should never have listened to you in the first place and hired this—this *loser*."

Brian hoped his feelings weren't showing. "Well," he said, taking a deep breath, "I guess I'd better leave." He headed for the door. Casey called out, "Wait!" But Brian was too upset to hear.

As the door closed, Casey swung on her father. "You're making a big mistake, Dad. I know for a fact that Brian is just about ready with a security system that will—. Well, it'll be the biggest thing to hit the industry ever. It'll knock you off your feet!"

"That boy has already just about knocked this company off its feet," R.J. said angrily. "And I don't want to hear any more about Brian Foster, either." He reached for the phone. "I'm calling the police."

For a second Casey stared at her father. Then, spinning on her heel, she stomped out of the office, slamming the door as hard as she could.

She stomped all the way to the elevator and stood there fuming. Just as it arrived and the doors opened, Ken Sharp came sprinting down the hall. "Hold it, Casey," he yelled.

Casey stepped inside. Sharp made it almost as the doors were sliding shut. "Maybe I can help," he panted.

Casey shook her head. "Thanks, Ken. But you know how stubborn my father can be."

Ken touched her elbow. "Look. Have dinner with me tonight. If Brian's got a new system, maybe I can figure out a way of getting your father to look at it. You know, give Brian another chance."

Casey shook her head. "Thanks, Ken. But not tonight. If I know Brian, he's probably inventing some new way to end it all right this minute."

The elevator stopped. Doors opened and Casey rushed out.

4

Casey brought her car to a screeching halt in front of Brian's house. Barely returning Mrs. Fowler's friendly wave, she dashed up the path and into the house.

"Brian! Where are you, Brian?" There was no reply. Heart pounding, she headed for the basement door. "Probably in his workshop," she muttered. "Oh, I hope he hasn't *done* anything."

Not only had Brian not done anything, he wasn't *doing* anything. Looking as though the world had already come to an end, Brian sat on a high stool staring down at his workbench.

Casey breathed happily once more. It was her first glimpse of the workshop. Technical books and magazines were stacked on shelves, built-in cubbyholes contained electronic equipment and working tools. But this was no time to show an interest in the furnishings.

Brian thumped a soldering iron gloomily. "What's up?" he asked in a dull, don't-much-care voice.

"My temper! That's what's up!" Casey exclaimed angrily. "I'm furious! I'll never forgive my father. Never in a hundred years! He shouldn't have treated you that way."

Brian sighed. "Uh...slow down, Casey. You can't blame him for—"

"Can't *blame* him? What kind of man would fire his future son-in-law?"

Brian gasped. "Casey! You mean you went ahead and told him we want to get married?"

"Well, why on earth shouldn't I? We do, don't we?"

"But we agreed that—"

Casey interrupted. "Okay. I *didn't* tell him. But I *will*. As soon as I get home. And not only that, but..."

Brian's kiss cut off information on Casey's further plans, and for the next few moments she forgot them herself.

"Look, Casey," Brian spoke gently into his fiancée's ear. "I don't think this is the best time to tell your father about our plans. First of all —you know how he feels about me right now. And second — you know how he's always felt about Ken Sharp."

Casey pushed away. "Then let *him* marry Ken!"

"Listen, Casey—with his business going to pot because of my security system not working, he isn't being unfair. What I can't understand is why it *isn't* working. I've checked and rechecked. To tell you the truth, if it weren't for my *new* security system—and the fact that I'm already fired — I'd quit!"

Casey didn't argue. She looked straight at Brian. "Tell me something, Brian—when will you be finished with this brilliant new system, anyway?"

Brian grinned. "Interested in seeing it?"

Casey's eyes sparkled. "It's *ready*? Why didn't you tell me? Show me! *Show* me!"

"Okay, Casey." Brian turned toward a door that opened into a closet, and called, "Forty-nine!"

Casey frowned. "Forty-nine what?"

"Watch." Brian's smile broadened. He flung out an arm. "Ta-DA!"

Out strolled Chomps. He glanced at Casey, sat down, and stared over at Brian.

"Well — what do you think?" the former Securities Head asked.

Casey looked puzzled. "What do I think of what?"

Brian pointed to Chomps. "What do you think of my new security system?"

Casey's frown deepened. "Rascal? Brian—I don't get it."

"You will," her fiancée replied cheerfully. "Watch." He looked down at Chomps. "Seventeen," he said loudly.

Chomps rolled over.

"Twenty-two," Brian ordered.

Chomps lifted four paws and played dead.

"Sixty-six!"

At this magical number, Chomps sat up and looked at Brian.

"Well, Casey — what do you think?" Brian asked.

Casey tried to find just the right reply. Maybe Brian's mind had been jolted by the day's events. She swallowed. "Well, he's the best trained dog in town, I guess. But what's your new invention?"

Brian pointed down. "That's it," he answered gleefully.

"*That*'s it? *Rascal?*"

"Nope." He whistled. A moment later Rascal came bounding joyfully into the workshop. "*That*'s Rascal," said Brian.

Casey stared. Rascal walked over and sat down beside his look-alike. She gasped, "Then who is that? Brian! They're like two bookends!"

Brian beamed. "That, my beautiful Casey, is my new security system." He snapped his fingers. "Forty-eight!"

Immediately the new security system leaped from the floor to the workbench. Rascal looked on with interest at this performance, but didn't seem at all jealous of his twin.

Chomps eyed Casey and she eyed him. His eyes took on a soft, reddish glow.

"Brian!" she gasped. "Something's *wrong* with that dog!"

"Something's right!" Brian said happily. "Three years' work, Casey. There it is! Three years of no new car, no new almost everything. You're looking at my big investment — Chomps."

"Chomps?"

"Yep, C.H.O.M.P.S. Chomps for short. Stands for Canine HOMe Protection System. An electronic watchdog. Computerized, self-activating, movable — a crime-stopper unlike any *watchdog* that ever existed."

Casey looked doubtful. "But what could that

little thing do to a burglar? Roll over on him?"

Brian laughed. "Chomps is a completely programmed security system. He can do a lot more than roll over. Trust me, Casey."

Putting an arm around Miss Casey Norton, Brian kissed her. And not forgetting Rascal, he patted his head. Casey kissed Brian. And not forgetting Chomps, patted the new home security system on *its* head.

Back at his office, R.J. was still pacing and fuming. Ken Sharp tried following him back and forth.

"But, R.J., we *need* something really extraordinary to turn things around for Norton Industries. If Foster really has come up with a revolutionary new system, we can't afford to pass it up."

Norton spun around. "I told you, and I'll tell you again. I'm not *interested*. I —"

A ring of the phone stopped him. He picked it up. "Who?" he asked, almost growling. "*Gibbs?*" He rolled up his eyes and sighed heavily. He was in no mood to talk with President Gibbs of Gibbs Guardian Corporation — his biggest competitor. "Listen, Gibbs, I know why you're calling, and I don't want to go

26

through it all again. I've had a tough morning."

Gibbs, comfortably dressed in a warmup suit, kept pedaling away on his exercise bicycle as he held the phone. "Well, I guess it *is* tough having your office broken into — especially when you manufacture burglar alarms." He laughed loudly. "I picked up the report on the police calls."

R.J. cut in. "As I said — I know what you're going to say next, so let me save you the trouble. The answer *is* and always *will be* — NO. I am NOT selling!"

"Be sensible, Ralph. You're in big trouble. I know what's been happening with your newest system. Everybody in the business knows."

Gibbs voice crackled on and R.J. glanced desperately at Ken Sharp. Ken didn't look desperate at all. He seemed to be admiring his fingernails.

A sudden idea flashed into R.J.'s head. *Brian Foster's new invention! My last hope!*

"Listen, Gibbs — you're in for a big surprise! You and everybody else in the business will be *obsolete — way* behind the time! Because what nobody knows is that my brilliant chief engineer has just come up with a new system that'll revolutionize the entire industry!"

Ken Sharp suddenly forgot his fascinating hands. He stared up in amazement.

"Just a second, Gibbs," R.J. said. "I'm putting on my Vice President in charge of Production. *He'll* tell you."

Ken Sharp gulped. "You've changed your mind?" he asked, keeping his voice low.

R.J. covered the phone receiver with his hand. "Not on your life. I just had to have *something* to say to that vulture. Now take the phone and tell him I'm not bluffing."

"But —"

"*Do* it."

Flustered, Ken Sharp took the phone. "Mr. Gibbs," he said firmly, "Mr. Norton is not bluffing."

R.J. grabbed back the phone and slammed it down. "Now *Gibbs* can start worrying."

5

In Brian's workshop Casey tried to follow the unbelievable story of Chomps' creation.

"At first," said Brian, "I started out to build a Doberman. Pretty successful, too. But not practical. I wanted a warning system, not necessarily a dead burglar. So I settled on Rascal as a model because of the 'surprise' factor."

Casey bent down to pat Chomps' head. "I get it. Who'd ever suspect a little fellow like you of being a ferocious watchdog? Right, Rascal?"

Rascal ducked his head between Chomps and Casey's hand. "Oh!" Casey exclaimed. "*That* was Chomps! Brian, how do you ever tell them apart?" She picked up Rascal.

Brian grinned. "I'm proud to say it's difficult. But when Chomps is operational you can hear a low hum."

Casey listened. "Right. I can."

"Eighty-six, Chomps."

Immediately, the hum ceased and Chomps became motionless. Brian lifted the revolutionary security system up to the workbench. "I'll show you the control system."

Rascal watched with great interest as Brian revealed Chomps' unusual insides. Small lights flashed on and off and tapes whirred.

"See, Casey — it's an exact duplicate of a canine central nervous system. It's activated by this highly sophisticated mini-computer. These circuits duplicate all five senses. Electronic impulses give Chomp superhearing, supersight — he has X-ray vision, in fact. And he has superspeed and strength."

Casey was a little pale. There was something too strange about viewing an open side panel on Rascal's double. "And he can't get hurt?" she asked a bit shakily.

Brian shook his head. "This outer shell is made of a nearly indestructible material I've developed." He closed the panel. "What d'you think?"

"I think you're a genius," Casey said promptly.

Rascal scrambled down from Casey's lap and trotted off to a favorite plastic bone. He brought it back to the workbench.

"I think Rascal wants to play, Brian."

Brian shook his head. "That's one of the few things Chomps doesn't do. On the other hand, he doesn't shed and he doesn't require feeding or walks."

"Do you think Rascal thinks Chomps is a dog?"

Brian grinned. "Rascal's too smart for that. Besides, he's in love with Muffin next door. He spends most of his time at Mrs. Fowler's house. That's when I got the idea of *building* a watchdog. And now, look! I'm just about ready to go into production. Chomps is the perfect watchdog."

As Chomps was being so highly congratulated, a black van was slowing to a stop just past Brian's house. Bracken was at the wheel and talking into a CB radio. "Okay, Pussycat, we're at the address now." He consulted a CB dictionary. "Clean and green," he said, and looked in the dictionary again. "We'll 10-22 you later. Good-bye."

"Now what does all that mean?" Brooks growled.

"'Green and clean' means everything is clear and '10-22' means we'll report to him in person." He paused. "And then I said good-bye."

"Yeah, yeah. *That* I got."

The pair got out of the van and made their way along the bushes between Brian's and Mrs. Fowler's house.

"There's the basement window," Brooks pointed. "That's where Foster's workshop is supposed to be."

Suddenly he grabbed Bracken's arm and tugged him into the bushes.

Mrs. Fowler's voice reached them all too clearly. "Now, Muffin — don't you run away this time." She set the little Peke on the front porch. Muffin lost no time in starting down the steps and into the yard.

"Muffin, did you hear me?" Mrs. Fowler asked sternly.

Muffin gave a short bark which evidently meant "yes," as Mrs. Fowler went back into the house.

Brooks and Bracken speedily went to Brian's side of the bushes, edging close to the basement window.

In the workshop Brian was lifting Chomps

down from the workbench. "And best of all, Casey," he said proudly, "Chomps is so easy to operate. All it takes to activate him from 'housedog' to 'watchdog' is the command — 'Twenty-one.'"

Chomp looked up, freezing in one position for a moment as tapes changed on the computer. He then turned to stare directly toward the basement window.

"What's he looking at, Brian?" Casey asked, puzzled. "Look at his eyes. They're turning bright red."

"Maybe he's just getting his bearings," Brian replied.

No sooner had he spoken than Chomps made a giant leap from the floor to the window. Glass smashed. Bricks flew.

Brian snatched Casey's hand. "His X-ray vision! Let's go! He's onto something!"

Brooks and Bracken could not have been more astonished if an elephant instead of a small rumpled-looking dog had crashed almost at their feet. But when Chomps growled ferociously and bared very white, very sharp teeth, the team of Brooks and Bracken made a dash for the only safe place in sight—a sizeable tree in the backyard.

"Up!" yelled Brooks.

"*Way* up!" yelled Bracken.

High in the leafy branches they looked down at Chomps, who'd reached the base of the tree a second too late to take off Bracken's sneakers —or possibly his pants. But, programmed for action, Chomps was not giving up. The sound of an enormous *chop* reached all the way to the high branches. The tree trembled.

Bracken, his eyes squeezed tight shut in fear, asked, "Is he leaving?"

"No. I think *we* are," Brooks replied desperately. *"The tree*'s *going over*."

"Whooooooo!!!" And on that sad departing note, the songbirds Brooks and Bracken found themselves sailing downward toward the neighboring backyard. And as the falling tree trunk whacked down on the dividing fence, the pair were shaken from their leafy nests—alas —right into a swimming pool. Small whitecaps closed over their heads!

"I don't know what went wrong!" Brian gasped. "He was only programmed for 'watchdog,' and he took off as though I'd given him the strongest signal."

"What's that?" Casey asked.

"I can't say it now," Brian replied. "He might take off again."

They looked past the now motionless Chomps and peered over the fence. "Nothing here," Brian said. "It must have been some malfunction. I'll program him for 'housedog' until I can check out his circuitry."

"That word!" Casey exclaimed. "Why can't you just say 'circuits'? It'd be a lot easier. Cir-Q-it-tree. It's so *complicated*, Brian."

"Circuitry-circuits. What's the difference?" Brian sighed. "Something went wrong. Twelve, Chomps."

Chomps clicked into action. Calmly he walked over to Brian's sneakers without even a backward look at the fence.

Brooks and Bracken, who had been gasping up, then down, in the pool, gasped up and swam for shore. "The van!" Brooks panted. "Let's get out of here."

So as Brian, Casey, and Chomps went back into the house to calm a wildly barking Rascal, the soggy pair managed to make it unnoticed to the van.

But Casey heard the loud revving-up of the van's engine. "Listen! Brian! Somebody *was* here. A burglar! It could have been a real burglar! Chomps *does* work."

Brian listened as the van took off, tires

squealing. "I hope you're right."

Casey bounced in excitement. "You've *got* to show this to Dad!"

"I can't, Casey. I'm not sure all the bugs have been worked out."

Casey waved her arms. "You mean fleas? What dog doesn't have fleas? Nonsense! Chomps is *terrific*." Excitedly she picked up Chomps, kissed Brian, and hugged both the inventor and the invention.

Chomps didn't have even a tail wag in return for all this love. But Rascal jumped up and down, determined to have his share of any hugs going around.

"Brian — look. Rascal's jealous!"

Brian bent down and scratched Rascal behind the ears—something Rascal rated higher than a hug. "That's something else I couldn't build into Chomps—love."

Casey smiled. "Well, Rascal has enough love for all four of us. Right?"

Mrs. Fowler could suddenly be heard. "Muffin? Muffin? Now where *does* she go?"

Brian chuckled. "Rascal has enough love for all *five* of us, Casey. Don't forget Muffin!"

Mrs. Fowler blew her trusty dog whistle.

Instantly Chomps lifted his head. His ears

perked up. "What's the matter, Chomps?" Brian asked.

Chomps' eyes glowed red as the high-pitched whistle affected his circuits. He took off like a runaway locomotive, straight through the house, on through the front door and into the street.

"We've got to catch him!" Brian shouted, already galloping out of the house after his disappearing revolutionary invention.

Casey caught up with him at the street curb. "Which way did he go?" she panted.

Brian pointed to a tipped-over fire hydrant at the corner of the block. Torrents of water spouted up from it. The corner stop sign was also lying flat on the ground. "Offhand," he gasped, "I'd say *that* way." Luckily, Casey's parked car was pointed in that direction.

"Jump in," she yelled.

This time Rascal did not intend to be left out of any possible adventure. He leaped into Brian's lap and the three zoomed off.

Up ahead, beyond the intersection, came a tremendous splintering sound. Out from the center of a billboard came Chomps, strips of advertising draped over his nose like banners in the wind.

Seeing this display, the driver of a passing car could really not be blamed for taking his eyes off traffic. As he crashed into the car ahead, Chomps sailed right over the hood.

A policeman heard the explosive sound of metal on metal and whirled around. "Tailgating!" he exclaimed. "When will they ever learn?" He blew an angry blast on his whistle.

Chomps' delicate circuits caught the high, piercing signal. He came to a stop—a stop on a dime! Instantly, the red lights in his glowing eyes faded as he returned to "housedog" programming.

He turned jauntily toward home, sparing only a moment to view the policeman writing out a traffic ticket. The driver, still speechless, gazed groggily at this passing picture of four-footed innocence.

Chomps was trotting quietly along the sidewalk when Casey spotted him.

"Forty-eight!" Brian yelled.

Chomps turned. Then, nice-as-you-please, he took his place beside Rascal for the homebound trip.

Brian frowned gloomily. "That's an example of those 'bugs' I was talking about, Casey. I've checked and rechecked, but so far I haven't found out what triggers this kind of action. It's happened a couple of times."

But Casey's spirits were high. "You know you'll work it out, Brian. Meantime, you've just *got* to let Dad see this!"

Outside a phone booth two streets away, Brooks and Bracken were searching their sodden pockets for coins. After a struggle, Bracken managed to find and drag out some change.

"Give it to me," Brooks demanded.

"Uh-*uh*! You said *I* could report in to Pussyfoot this time."

"Some report!" Brooks snorted. "A dog chased us off before we could find anything."

"Well—*that's* a report, isn't it?" He clinked coins into the slot and began dialing.

"Hurry up," Brooks said. "It's cold out here."

"Got the answering service. I only got twenty seconds to leave a message."

"Then *talk*, dummy."

"Can't. They told me to wait for the dial tone."

Brooks tapped a squishy shoe. Bracken lifted his hand. "Got it!"

"Talk."

"Foxy One reporting in. Went to address as instructed. Scouted — A-aa-aa-Choo!"

"Gesundheit." Brooks' voice could be heard in the background.

"Thanks," Bracken said politely.

"Just keep talking. The time's almost up," Brooks urged.

"Now let me see—where was I? Pussyfoot?"

There was a CLICK. At the other end of the line "Pussyfoot" (known to R.J. Norton as Ken Sharp) fumed. Pressing a button, he turned the machine off and sank back in his desk chair, groaning loudly. "Those idiots!" He exclaimed. "Now what'll I tell Gibbs?"

6

Casey parked her sportscar in the driveway beside her father's long gleaming limousine and hurried into the Norton mansion. She found her father behind his desk in the library, staring gloomily at rows of books.

"Dad, you just *have* to listen. I've just seen Brian's new security system. And you've never seen anything like it in your life. You just have to —"

R.J. raised his hand. "Not interested, Casey. I never want to have anything to do with Brian — or any other young computer 'geniuses.' *Never*. Forget him and his nutty idea."

"It's not nutty!" his daughter said hotly. "It's revolutionary."

"Even worse," her father sighed. "Whatever it is, it's nutty. Forget him. Ken Sharp is the one for you. He's the best man I have."

"Look, Dad..." Casey tried to keep her voice calm. "I might as well tell you. I've already invited Brian over."

R.J. jumped up. *"Here? Good-bye!* I'll sneak out the back door."

"Dad —" Casey called after him.

Her father moved swiftly to the back of the mansion and flung open the kitchen door.

"Good evening, Mr. Norton," said Brian Foster, smiling. He motioned to the dog carrier he held. "I've —"

"I'll use the front door," R.J. said. SLAM.

Casey sped into the kitchen. "Dad, you get back here. You're acting like a child."

R.J. stopped. "Show me a child with a five-million-dollar business on the edge of bankruptcy," he said.

Casey turned the doorknob. "Brian — come in."

Brian set the dog carrier down. R.J. could see the letters C.H.O.M.P.S. painted on the side.

"I want you to know I'm here under protest, Foster," he said, folding his arms.

"And I understand that, sir," Brian replied. "But if you'll just give me a chance to show you —"

"All right! All right! Show it to me and I'll tell you it's a nutty idea. And then you can go collect unemployment insurance. Well! Where is it? I don't have much time."

Brian shot an uneasy glance at Casey. He bent down and opened the front of the dog carrier. "Well, sir — it's in here."

"What is? A new gong? Electric eyes? An unpickable lock?"

"Not quite," Brian said. He turned to the carrier and spoke sharply. "Twenty-one!"

A low hum sounded. Out stepped Chomps. He looked coolly around the kitchen, paying no real attention to anything or anybody.

Norton's eyes widened. "Is this your idea of a joke, Foster? That's your dog."

"No, sir. Not Rascal. It's —"

"Hmmph! 'Rover' I suppose. Foster, *that's* your 'revolutionary development'? If I've seen that dog *one* time, I've seen him *one hundred* times!"

Chomps' eyes built up to a red glow. There was a low whirring sound followed by a CLICK—and R.J. Norton found himself suddenly pinned to the kitchen floor looking up into Chomps' red eyes.

Between shock and anger, R.J. found it hard to keep his voice steady. "Foster, I'm going to be very calm about this. I don't know what you're up to. BUT—I'm giving you three seconds to get this mutt off my chest!"

"One second will be plenty, sir," said Brian, re-programming Chomps.

For the first time, a faint interested light came into R.J. Norton's eyes. "Well," he said gruffly. "I suppose you're not going to go away until you've made a speech. So 'speech' away, Foster. But make it fast."

Outside, in the deepening dusk, a van cruised past the Norton driveway. The driver put on the brakes. "You see what I see?" asked the driver.

"Yep. A lot of nice spare parts," his companion answered. "Very nice *expensive* spare parts."

"Let's go," the driver grinned. "It'll be a quick hit."

Expertly the van was backed up the drive to the deep shade of overhanging trees. The two thieves jumped out. They swung open the van rear doors, reached in for tools—and seconds later were hard at work jacking up the Cadillac, wrenching off the wheels, prying out dashboard equipment, and emptying the trunk of spare tire and tools.

In the mansion, the "conference" had moved from the kitchen to the library, and Chomps was standing, de-activated, on R.J.'s desk.

"...and each operation of the Canine Home Protection System..." said Brian, pointing to the complicated circuitry in the side panel.

"That's 'Chomps' for short," Casey interrupted quickly.

"...each operation is triggered by a numerical command."

R.J. frowned. "You mean, for instance, if I said 'one-hun—"

Brian clapped a hand over his former boss's mouth. "Right! That number triggers his 'karate' jump." He closed the panel.

R.J. leaned back, hands folded across his stomach.

"Well — what do you think, Dad?" asked Casey.

"It's amazing. But really—how much could a little dog like that do? Even an *electronic* little dog?"

Brian spoke eagerly. "Well, when Chomps is activated for 'watchdog,' as he is now, he can sense a prowler anywhere within one thousand yards."

R.J. shrugged. "That's what you *say*."

"Dad, will you please listen? Go on, Brian."

Brian nodded. "His first reaction is to zero in on the suspect area," he said, looking at R.J.

If he'd been looking at Chomps, instead, he'd have seen two eyes starting to glow. He went on. "His first reaction is to zero in on the suspect area. Next his visual sensors confirm the suspect area. Then —"

"Brian! Look! Chomps is 'suspecting' this minute!" Casey cried.

Sure enough! Chomps' X-ray vision was focused beyond the wall to the driveway. In a great forward leap he started out pell-mell. Clearing a sofa in a single bound, he raced from the library, tore down the hall, shot through the kitchen sending chairs flying, and smashed his way out the door leading to the garage.

Before R.J., Casey, and Brian could catch up, they heard the smashing crunch of Chomps slamming straight through the closed garage doors. He headed straight for the van.

Two thunderstruck thieves slammed the

van doors shut. They leaped to safety in the nick of time. "Did you see that!" gasped the driver. "The dog came through *solid* doors." He revved the engine and shot down the driveway, tires shrieking. Chomps raced behind, barely one nip away.

Brian hadn't expected Chomps would be giving a demonstration at the first interview and he was delighted. "Look!" he cried. "Chomps is chasing a car!"

R.J. Norton sneered. "Now that *is* an original invention. It could make headlines—DOG CHASES CAR."

"Dad!"

"Come on," her father said. "We might as well catch them." He jumped behind the wheel of his Cadillac. He gunned the motor to a roar, but the big car was going nowhere. "*Now* what!" he said furiously. "Why won't this car *move*?"

Brian stretched sideways to peer at the wheels. "No wheels, sir," he reported. "You're up on jacks."

"My car! We'll take my car!" Casey yelled. "Dad — move over. Let me out! We'll lose 'em!"

All three piled into the sportscar and sailed

out the driveway. They reached the street just in time to see the van far up ahead make a left turn on Butler Avenue.

"After 'em, Casey!" yelled R.J.

The van was now speeding along Butler with Chomps bounding behind, nearly closing the gap.

"Step on it, willya?" the thief on the passenger side shouted. "That mutt is gaining on us."

"I got it to the floor now," the driver shouted back.

His companion groaned. "And now we got that sportscar tailing us!"

"I'll cut over and lose 'em on Elm," the driver snarled, bending over the wheel as if to help speed the van forward.

With a squeal of braking tires the van rocked into Elm Street.

"Hey, we lost him. The mutt's gone! He headed off on that vacant lot on the corner."

"Yeah! But look again, pal. Look what's up ahead!"

At the intersection of Butler and Main, sawhorses formed a barricade across the right hand lane. A large sign spelled out DETOUR. That left only the lane open between the vacant lot and a gas station-repair garage across the street.

"The mutt's *taking a shortcut*," said the driver grimly.

As Chomps reached the corner the van was still bearing down toward the intersection. Without losing a second, Chomps grabbed the nearest sawhorse in his jaws, blocking the open lefthand lane.

There was only one way to go and the van driver took it — straight up the repair garage driveway. And before the astonished gaze of the attendant who was closing for the night, it came to a screeching stop — on the hydraulic lift.

Like a tornado, Chomps rushed up. Standing on his short hind legs, he grabbed the lift lever in his powerful jaws and pulled it to "ON" position.

The hoods were only halfway out the van doors when they saw that the concrete flooring seemed to be sinking below them. "Hey! We're going up!" cried the driver. "*And it's that dog again.* Get your legs back in! Shut your door."

At that moment the van roof crunched into the ceiling. As it flattened, the doors buckled and jammed tight. The two occupants couldn't have been better locked-in if they were in the Hamilton slammer!

Outside a car whizzed up, and when Brian and the Nortons got out, Chomps was sitting innocently by the lift control lever. "Forty-eight, Chomps!" Brian yelled.

With a gentle leap, Chomps bounded into Brian's arms, and then came the sound of police sirens and the excited voices of spectators.

"What's going on here, anyway?" a policeman yelled above the crowd of onlookers and the slamming thuds from the van.

"It was that dog," the garage attendant babbled excitedly. "That little dog did it all. He pushed the lever and rammed them in the ceiling."

By this time a mobile TV unit had arrived, the cameraman taking it all in, and a reporter elbowing his way to the center of the excitement. "Excuse me. Excuse me. Scott Elliot, KDEP NEWS. Did I hear him say that dog *did all this*?"

Brian held Chomps close as the reporter thrust a microphone forward. "I — ."

But R.J. Norton grabbed it away.

"That's right," he said proudly. "But this

isn't just *any* dog. This is part of a new, top-secret security project that we at Norton Industries are developing."

Brian started to speak but R.J. motioned him aside. "As you may know," he went on, "Norton Industries has long been the leader in supplying security and alarm systems to the citizens of Hamilton. In fact — nationally."

"What about the dog, sir?" the reporter managed to ask.

But R.J. Norton didn't get this kind of advertising just any old day. He refused to give up the mike.

Casey grinned and squeezed Brian's hand. Chomps did nothing but rest comfortably on "forty-eight."

C.H.O.M.P.S. PHOTOS

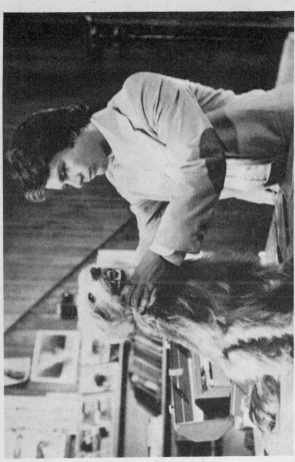

Wesley Eure as Brian Foster, a burglar-systems engineer and electronic genius, gives the finishing touch to his Canine HOMe Protection System — the super watchdog, Chomps.

This is Rascal, a lovable but undependable mutt; his raggedy shape is the model for C.H.O.M.P.S. Here, Rascal poses with Monster's bone.

Casey insists that her father, R.J. Norton (played by Conrad Bain), take a look at Brian's marvelous invention. Norton agrees, reluctantly.

Valerie Bertinelli plays Casey Norton, the boss's beautiful daughter. She knows Brian is a genius and intends to prove it to her father.

Things are looking rosy for the future Mrs. Brian Foster. But is Chomps *really* safe, or will burglars steal the world's best watchdog?

"A dog!" Norton exclaims. Even after R.J. is shown Chomps' complicated workings, he is still skeptical.

Brooks and Bracken, two bumbling burglars, played by Red Buttons and Chuck McCann, look terrified. They're supposed to seize Chomps for a business rival of Norton's — but Chomps is about to flatten them!

Chomps demonstrates his karate chop — right through a brick wall!

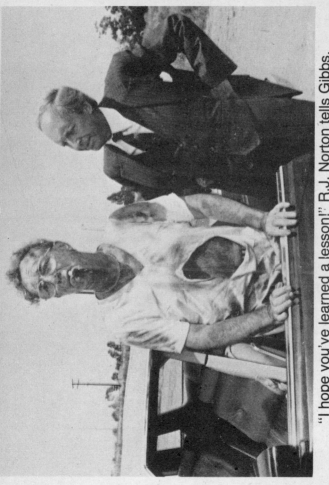
"I hope you've learned a lesson!" R.J. Norton tells Gibbs, a spying business rival, played by Jim Backus.

It's test time. Brian and Casey know Chomps will find the explosive in the York systems test — but will he come through okay?

Here, Rascal and the happy pair rejoice. Not only will Chomps be all right, but soon he'll have some electronic brothers!

7

Monday morning might have been twenty-four years instead of twenty-four hours from yesterday's Sunday emergency meeting.

R.J. Norton was beaming. Brian Foster was looking stunned — in happy surprise — and Ken Sharp was reeling in shock. R.J. had just said, "And so, Sharp, I'd like you to meet Norton Industries' future Vice-President in Charge of Systems Development."

A bright smile suddenly spread over the future Vice President's face. "And may I add, sir... your future son-in-law?"

"You may," R.J. replied graciously.

Ken Sharp nearly jumped. "Vice Presi — ?

Son-in-law?" He tried to keep fury out of his face and voice. "Uh—what happened between yesterday and today?"

"A revolution, Sharp," R.J. replied joyfully. "A revolution! With one fell swoop, Foster here has revolutionized the entire security systems industry."

"You mean that 'incredible invention' you mentioned yesterday, Brian?"

"Well, I . . . uh . . ."

R.J. clapped his hands together. "Even *more* incredible! It's beyond incredible. It's . . . it's . . . . "

"Revolutionary?" Ken Sharp asked, already knowing R.J. would agree.

"Exactly! You've suggested the right word, Ken," said R.J. "And after a test I've just set up for tonight at Merkel's Department Store, success will be in the bag!"

"Well, what is it?"

"You'll soon see! Foster has set up a special pre-demonstration in a parking lot. We'll take a run over there now and then you'll understand what I've been talking about."

In a closed area of the parking lot, a tall ladder had been placed up against a second-story window of the main building.

So far, Ken Sharp hadn't spotted anything that looked like an alarm device anywhere on the building. And when Brian and R.J. arrived he didn't intend to ask any questions about the "revolutionary invention," either.

R.J. was already beaming in delight as he and Brian came rolling into the parking lot in R.J.'s Cadillac. Brian stepped out of the car, then reached back for the dog carrier.

Ken Sharp laughed. "I see you didn't want your dog to miss the big event, Foster."

"Sure didn't," Brian answered proudly. He opened the carrier and took out Chomps. "My 'dog' is the big event."

Sharp stared. "*That's* the new security system? You've got to be joking!"

"It's no joke," R.J. said. "Sharp, the Canine Home Protection System—'Chomps' for short —is the biggest thing since the lock."

Brian nodded. "The demonstration should answer a lot of your questions, Ken."

He led the group toward the ladder. "We set up this first test to show how effective Chomps can be in preventing the break-in of a second-story man."

Ken sneered. "That little dog is going to stop a burglar? Come on, Foster."

Chomps looked up, cute and innocent as Rascal. And Ken Sharp looked down. "Let *me* be the second-story man. He doesn't scare *me*."

"Now wait a minute —"

Ken had already jumped up on the second rung of the ladder. Brian moved to stop him, but R.J. moved to stop Brian. "He *insists*, Foster. Let him go ahead."

Halfway up and still climbing, Ken Sharp called back. "Okay. Okay. I'm the burglar. So what?"

"You heard him, Foster," R.J. grinned.

Brian sighed. "Well — if you insist. Here goes. *Sixty-one!*"

Chomps eyes glowed red. A second later he was off like a flash. He leaped, grabbed one side of the ladder in his jaws and gave his head a shake.

"Hey!" Sharp called down. "Hold it! This thing is wobbling."

SNAP! Chomps' jaws crunched. All along the length of the ladder the rungs parted like a split wishbone. Sharp, now looking like a man on giant-size stilts, wobbled desperately.

"YEOWW!" Over he toppled, jack-knifing into a fairly well-padded trashcan.

"Nice going, Chomps!" Norton yelled. He leaned over Sharp. "*Now* what do you think?"

"I think the ladder broke," Sharp snapped.

"That was no accident," Norton gloated. "That was C-H-O-M-P-S, Chomps."

Brian helped Ken to his feet. "The purpose of this demonstration is to show that the Canine Home Protection System can adapt to any crime."

Sharp brushed excelsior shavings off his trousers. "Well, I think it demonstrated that you've slipped your gears, Foster."

Angrily he stepped over and into his car. He leaned out the window. "In fact, it will be a pleasure to help prove it to you. You can just tell that mutt I've suddenly become a car-thief." The "thief" whizzed up the motor to a roar.

"You asked for it," Brian muttered. "Chomps — fifty-six!"

Like an arrow in flight, Chomps leaped from the ground to the car trunk and up once more to the roof. Getting a good grip at the front edge, he ripped back. And suddenly Ken Sharp looked like a lonely sardine left in a rolled-back sardine can. Dazed, he brought the car to a stop. Through the rear-view mirror he could see Chomps calmly eyeing him from his perch on the trunk.

Brian rushed up. "Are you hurt?" he asked anxiously.

"Never mind that," R.J. said. "Well, what do you think of Chomps now, Sharp?"

Ken Sharp clutched the steering wheel with white-knuckled hands. "I — I think I'd really like to go home now and — and, *think*."

Still dazed, he drove out of the parking lot, mumbling to himself. "An electronic watchdog. Is it possible? And they're testing tonight at Merkel's Department Store! *I've got to contact Gibbs!*" He sped on down the road.

When R.J. Norton's rival, President of the Gibbs' Guardian Systems, flipped on the morning TV newscast he had no idea his day was about to be ruined.

"For those who missed our earlier news flash, here is a repeat of our coverage of an attempted robbery that was foiled last night," said the announcer. On screen came Chomps, held in Brian Foster's arm. R.J. stood proudly at Brian's elbow.

"Yes, ladies and gentlemen — foiled by this super watchdog. Perhaps Mr. Norton here—"

"Of Norton Industries," R.J. added quickly.

"—the owner of this remarkable animal can explain how it all happened." The reporter held out the mike to R.J.

As R.J. rushed into explaining the new Canine Home Protection System, Gibbs began to burn. And the more Norton said the more furious Gibbs became.

"Chomps, as we call this revolutionary invention for short," Norton beamed, "will soon be available to every home owner and businessman in the country."

The reporter pulled back the mike. "Well, I'd say that dog is one in a hundred!"

Hundred! Too late, Brian and Norton grabbed at Chomps. The reporter toppled backward as Chomps made his usual great karate leap.

"Eighty-six! Eighty-six!" Brian yelled.

Norton helped the dazed reporter to his feet. "You activated his karate jump," he explained to the reporter — and to all TV viewers.

"Great dog!" the reporter babbled. "Great, great..."

Gibbs jumped to his feet and flipped off the TV switch. "That should have been MINE!" he yelled at the empty screen.

He was in no mood to speak pleasantly into the phone when it rang. "Yes!" he snarled.

"Mr. Gibbs," Ken Sharp said weakly, "wait 'til you hear this. I've found out what Norton's revolutionary new project is — a dog! I didn't believe it myself until I saw it demonstrated. But it can do *anything*!"

Gibbs burned on steadily, too enraged to speak.

Ken Sharp went on. "It's electronic but it looks absolutely real... and it's *top secret*."

Gibbs' burning fuse came to an end. "*Secret!*" he exploded. "Secret, did you say? Sharp, you dummy! It's so secret that I just saw it on *television*."

For the second time that morning, Ken Sharp was stunned.

"I want that dog, Sharp. I want that dog more than I've ever wanted *anything*. And I intend to *get* that dog! Do you read me?"

"Y-y-yes, sir."

"Your job hangs in the balance, Sharp," Gibbs grated. "What would Norton do if he found out you've been helping the competition to sabotage his systems?"

"I'd — I'd hate to think," Sharp quavered. "I'll get right on it, sir."

"Get on it, then. And GET IT!" He slammed down the phone.

Brooks and Bracken stepped into the hurry and bustle of the airlines terminal.

Looking nervously around as though to make certain they were not being followed, they spotted Ken Sharp in the end booth of a long line of telephones. Together, they moved to the opposite end. Brooks dug out a coin. "You stand guard," he told Bracken. Dialing the number of the far-end booth, he had barely a second to wait before Ken Sharp picked up the receiver. "Foxy two reporting —"

Ken cut him short. "Listen and listen close. The system is going to be tested tonight at Merkel's Department Store. Your assignment is to get it. Got it?"

"Look," said Foxy two," the only reason we showed up here is to tell you we're not going to show up anymore. If that dog is still guarding the system, we don't want no part of it."

Bracken, listening, nodded. "*No* part of it," he repeated.

"You dummies!" Sharp's voice rose to a shout. "That dog *is* the system. *And we want it!*"

Passersby glanced toward the booth. He

lowered his voice. "You want more money? We'll double your fee."

"Double?" Brooks looked up at Bracken. "They'll double our fee. What do you say?"

In reply, Bracken reached into the booth and pressed down the receiver button. "Ask for triple," he said grandly.

"Bracken! You cut us off. Gimme some change."

Bracken searched his pockets. "Sorry. All I got is a nickel."

"Then *get* some!" his partner demanded. "And don't attract attention."

Ken Sharp, furious at being cut off, waited for the phone to ring again. A hand came down on his shoulder. He jumped and turned to see Bracken decked out in a ski mask, standing over him.

"What do you think you're doing?" he raged.

"I'm trying to borrow phone money," Bracken replied.

"I mean — with the mask!"

Bracken looked right and left, then peeled it off. "Brooks said not to attract attention," he said obediently. "I think just a couple of dimes would cover it. Got 'em?"

Ken Sharp nearly ripped out the phone.

"Got 'em," he snarled. "But as long as you're here give me an answer. Double money for getting the dog tonight at Merkel's."

Bracken hesitated. "Okay — but make it triple."

"Okay," Ken agreed.

8

As the last of the evening customers swung through the revolving doors of Merkel's Department Store, the big lighted sign above the eighth floor of the building blinked off.

Inside, employees were getting ready to go home—except for a lone security guard whose "day's work" was usually just beginning. It was not long before he would be the only one left in the big building — or so he thought.

To make sure no one would be trapped in the store for the night, the guard began a security check. One half hour later he had made a last and final check of the restrooms, then headed for the first floor, wondering why he and five police dogs had been given the night off.

Brooks and Bracken, on the other hand, were thinking of the long wait they'd had in the restroom before they could begin *their* night's work. It had been no fun balancing on the plumbing pipes while the guard checked for pairs of feet that would betray their uncomfortable hideout.

Finally, Brooks called out in a loud whisper, "Okay, Bracken. The coast is clear. Get out the canvas sack. Let's get that dog."

"Where'll he be?" Bracken asked.

"Don't worry. He'll find *us*. Just be ready for him."

At the store's front entrance, the guard stepped out, joining the group by the door. "Okay, Mr. Merkel," he said. "Store's empty."

Mr. Jonathan Merkel, owner and founder of the store, thanked him, then turned to Brian and R.J. Norton. He looked down at Chomps, standing motionless at Brian's feet. "I want you to know, Norton, that I think you've lost your mind. How can you tell me this little dog will protect my store when your alarm system and five police dogs couldn't?"

R.J. smiled. "It's just as I said, Jonathan. I can't *tell* you why. It's top secret — but remember, I'll personally make good any losses you might have."

Mr. Merkel shook his head. "It's your money."

R.J. turned to Brian. "Go ahead, Brian, turn Chomps loose."

Brian activated Chomps to "watchdog." "Okay, Chomps. This is your big chance. Twenty-one!"

Chomps eyes began to glow and a loud CLICK could be heard as he was re-programmed. He trotted past the guard as the door was held open for him. They watched him disappear behind a counter.

"You can lock up now," Mr. Merkel told his employee, and then watched as the main door was bolted securely.

"Jonathan, you needn't worry tonight," R.J. said. "Foster here will be monitoring this new system from his car. So we're on top of any problem all the way. See?"

Mr. Merkel shrugged. "All I can see is another new system for going bankrupt. But good luck."

He and the guard left for the night. R.J. got into the Cadillac, and Brian joined Casey, who had been waiting in his car.

"Thanks, sir," Brian called out as he pulled away from the curb. "Goodnight."

"Goodnight, my boy," R.J. called back,

waving a hand as though giving the pair his blessing.

In the store, Chomps was already right on the job, trotting up and down each first floor aisle. He then set out for the second floor to continue his patrol.

Behind a counter crouched Brooks and Bracken. They could hear quick small pawsteps nearing them. "Okay," Bracken whispered. "Here he comes."

"Don't blow it!" Brooks warned.

Chomps suddenly stopped. His ears perked up. CLICK. He looked to the left. To the right. Just as he zeroed in on the signals his circuitry was picking up, Bracken acted! Down came the canvas bag, trapping an entire security system within!

Brooks and Bracken stood up in triumph. "We got 'im!" Bracken exclaimed. "It was apple pie and at *triple* the price!"

But Bracken was counting his pie before it was sliced. The bag in his hands went wild. If he hadn't *seen* the little dog, he would have sworn he was hanging on to a fighting mountain lion. "Help!" he shouted to Brooks.

Tearing, growling, slashing, Chomps fought two pairs of hands. And as the bag swung violently from side to side, Brooks and Bracken hung on with all their might. In vain! *They* began swinging from side to side, clinging desperately. They were no match for their four-footed opponent. And when Chomps made a jumping supertwist, both men lost their balance. Down went the bag, Chomps still inside. And slip-sliding along the floor went the unhappy Brooks and Bracken, crashing into glass counters.

In fear of their lives, they leaped to their feet. Chomps was just as fast. To the end of their days neither Brooks nor Bracken ever planned to say "It's in the bag!" That would have brought up too many sad memories. *The bag went leaping after them!*

Brian, behind the wheel of his car, couldn't remember when he had been so happy. Casey, next to him, was pretty happy, too. "How about that, Brian?" she giggled. "In one short day you get your job back and *we* get my father's blessing!"

"That's something all right," he grinned. "It's been quite a day."

"And now we've got the whole evening to ourselves."

Casey tried to slide over closer to Brian but something blocked the slide. "Ouch! Brian, I think something has just come between us!" She picked up a black boxlike object. It was easy to see what she'd bumped — a series of instrument gauges and buttons. "What is this?" she asked.

"Oh, that," he glanced at it for only a moment. "That's the C.H.O.M.P.S. monitoring system. With this I can keep tabs on Chomps wherever I am. As long as it doesn't start flashing or beeping, there's no problem."

Almost as he spoke the device flashed and beeped frantically. "There's a problem!" Casey exclaimed. "Or do you think maybe I sat on it?"

"Nope." Brian, tires squealing, made a sharp U-turn. "There's a problem all right." He raced back in the direction they'd come from.

On the second floor of Merkel's, Brooks and Bracken were still speeding only one jump ahead of the madly flapping bag.

"I don't get it," Brooks panted. "I don't get it. It's only a dog!"

"Tell that to the bag," Bracken puffed.

★ ★ ★

In the dark alley beside the store, a truck pulled up to a side door. Quickly, quietly, three men stepped out. It wouldn't have taken an expert to know they were up to no good.

Two of three stood guard at the doorway. The third man worked swiftly on the store's security system. Clipping just the right wires to disconnect the large alarm bell, it was only a matter of minutes before all three entered the store. They headed for the fur department.

Here again, was a job for an expert — opening the vault where racks of costly furs were stored. Losing no time, they began wheeling out a fortune in beautiful and expensive merchandise.

Brooks and Bracken were not having that kind of luck in their try at thievery. They were galloping up the long escalator stairs, thinking more about safety than stealing.

Below them, Chomps had just about shredded the canvas bag and would soon be wriggling out of it.

"UP! Up!" yelled Bracken at Brooks, who was already leaping upward three stairs at a time.

81

Almost free again, Chomps' eyes glowed hot red as he watched the pair on the stairs. Brooks, followed by Bracken, put on a burst of speed. And suddenly the pair found themselves in new territory — the sports department.

Another time they would have enjoyed, perhaps even tried out, some of the gym equipment. But now they were hardly in shape for further exercise. Besides, Chomps might show up any minute.

"The best thing is to pretend we're dummies," Bracken said.

"Pretend?" asked Brooks, scornfully. *"You* lost him."

But there was no time for exchanging insults. Brooks snatched up a baseball cap, plunked it on his head, then held up a tennis racket. He stepped up to a platform, pushed over a store dummy, and stood motionless. Bracken donned football shoulder pads, then selected a ski pole and a tennis racket to go with his borrowed outfit.

It was no wonder that Chomps *pinged* loudly as he spotted them. He came to a skidding stop from his run up the stairs and eyed them fiercely.

Much to their relief, Chomps seemed to

have no plans for biting them. But they watched fearfully as he trotted over to a tennis ball server machine. Putting a paw on the machine lever, Chomps set the server in motion *straight in the direction of the store's newest dummies.*

Tennis balls flew, hitting the pair from top to toe. With every stinging strike they tried to fight back with the borrowed rackets.

"WATCH IT!" Brooks shouted.

"DUCK!" Bracken shouted back.

But it was a battle lost and the crooks rushed away from the tennis ball blizzard. They crossed the department where a trampoline was set up. They leaped up on it, bouncing wildly back and forth while Chomps skidded to and fro beneath them.

"We-can't-keep-this-up-the-rest-of-our-lives," Brooks panted.

"We'd-better-make-a-run-for-it," Bracken panted back.

They bounded off — unfortunately, into a display of skateboards. Arms flailing, they went weaving frantically between counters, Chomps in hot pursuit.

Up ahead was a tent set up to advertise camping equipment. Its sheltering flaps with a glimpse of cots inside beckoned the exhausted skateboarders. Alas! Before they had time to pause for a well-deserved rest, they went shooting out the other end of the tent.

And this time what they saw ahead was so astonishing that Chomps was momentarily forgotten. The staircase! Down, down, down it went. In a split second the team of Bracken and Brooks would be taking the trip to the main floor in record time! But hanging from the ceiling right over the awesome descent was a colorful hang-glider. There was really no choice. Wide-eyed and frantic, they made a grab for it.

A worse fate than the stairs, or Chomps, awaited them. Pulled loose from the hooks, the glider went sailing across the entire width of the store toward a wall above a high window. It bumped the wall and CRA-A-ASH! Out through the window went Brooks and Bracken. *"Helllppp!"*

Chomps listened, looked up. Silence. Then a sound from below reached his ears. His tapes recycled. His X-ray vision took over. Down through the floors and out to the alley, he could plainly see the fur thieves loading the last of the furs into the truck.

Chomps zoomed downward, barely touching the stairs with his flying paws. At top speed he zeroed in on the side door. It flew off its hinges as Chomps burst through. Without stopping he raced down the alley, caught up as the truck turned into the street, and took a flying leap.

BIFF! Chomps balanced on the side as the truck tipped over into the street. One quick sprint forward and he was peering in the window of the overturned door. He could instantly see that if ever a door should be locked it was this one. Deftly seizing the door handle, he bit it into a tangled bend.

By the time Brian and Casey came whizzing to the scene, Chomps had once again created his own mobile slammer.

No sooner had Brian and Casey rushed to the overturned truck than a police car, red lights flashing, siren blaring, pulled to a screeching stop.

"Fantastic, Chomps! Fantastic!" Brian yelled.

Police jumped out. "What's going — FUR THIEVES! Look!" An officer pointed to the back of the truck. Mink coats and other beautiful furs were sliding to the ground.

"Right, officer!" Brian agreed. "And Chomps got 'em."

Chomps, his work done for the time, eyed

the scene airily from his high perch on the truck door.

The events at the Merkel Department Store had not quite ended, although the police, thieves, Brian, Casey, and Chomps were gone. As a result, they all missed the unbelievable scene when gray, chilly dawn broke.

In a huge trash container, far below a high window of the store, Brooks and Bracken huddled together, draped in all sorts of trash — crumpled wrapping paper, oily rags, and crate stuffings.

Bracken peered over the edge of the bin. "It's not so big a jump to the ground. Should we try it?"

"We've already come a long way," Brooks groaned, looking up at the high window. "Let's wait 'til it's lighter."

Bracken nodded. "Guess so." He shivered. "I sure would like to know what that Foster guy feeds his dog."

"Never mind the dog! What about our triple pay? What about *us*?"

"Us!" Bracken actually giggled. "Look at it this way, Brooks. What *more* could happen to us?"

The rumbling sound of a big truck reached

them and they ducked down. The truck came to a stop. Its fork clamped down on the big bin. Brooks and Bracken were lifted in the air.

TILT! DUMP! And a wild laugh came from the middle of the heaped-up load. "That's right, Bracken. What more *could* happen to us?"

9

R.J. Norton hardly had time to sit down at his desk before the first morning phone call came in. "Norton speaking," he said.

Ken Sharp, seated in his usual place, listened and watched a smile spread broadly across his boss's face.

"So!" R.J. exclaimed. "You've heard about what happened at Merkel's Department Store? I knew you would. So you know there's no chance for a merger with Gibbs Guardian or anything else! Give up, Gibbs! And now pardon me while I *hang* up!"

`He slapped down the phone and chuckled happily. "How do you like that? The minute somebody creates something great, the whole world wants a piece of it!"

Ken Sharp tried to look as though he were thinking hard. "I don't know, R.J. Maybe a merger with Gibbs Guardian wouldn't be such a bad idea. Gibbs has a lot to offer."

"Are you kidding?" R.J. guffawed. "Besides, I've already had another offer to merge!"

Ken Sharp's eyebrows rose. "Another offer! Who made it?"

R.J. stood up and began pacing the carpeting, shaking his fists in triumph. "York Systems!"

Ken Sharp was stunned. "*York Systems!*"

"Yes. And *they* called *me*! What do you think about that?"

R.J.'s second-in-command gulped. "I — I think it's absolutely fantastic, R.J."

Norton stopped his pacing long enough to bang a fist on the desk top. "You bet it's fantastic! York Systems, no less — only the biggest electronic systems conglomerate in the world. In the *world*, Sharp," he repeated. "Once they see Chomps in action, I'll be able to name my own terms."

Sharp suddenly became very businesslike. "We'll have to work up a really spectacular demonstration."

"It's already planned and arranged for, Sharp. But the place is top-secret. I've given them my word on that."

"Good thinking, R.J.," Sharp exclaimed. Then, much as he hated to say it, added, "This is one time we don't want any leaks!"

Casey Norton made her way through the noonday sidewalk traffic and turned into a small outdoor cafe, bright with umbrella-topped tables.

As she moved toward a table and seated herself, Ken Sharp moved quickly from the doorway where he had been waiting in the hope she'd appear. "Hi, Casey! This is a surprise!"

"Ken! Hi to you! Won't you sit down?"

"Thanks." Ken Sharp pulled back a chair. "Expecting Brian?" Casey smiled. "Of course."

Sharp smiled back. "There's no doubt about it, Casey. Brian is a genius. Your father was just telling me about the demonstration planned for York Systems today."

"Isn't it exciting?" Casey beamed.

"And big, too." Sharp nodded. "Who would ever expect we'd hold a demonstration..." He hesitated, but found the right word. "...there!"

"Oh, I agree, Ken," Casey replied. "Using the football field for the test has *got* to be impressive."

"Football field!" Quickly, Sharp covered his amazement. "Careful, Casey," he said hastily. "Don't go telling anyone about that. The word is — *tight* security. And that's where I come in." He leaned forward and pressed his hand over hers.

Brian strode up, his eye on Ken Sharp's hand. "Hi, Casey. Sorry I'm late."

"That's all right, Brian. Ken has been keeping me company."

Brian sat down and nodded stiffly. "Thanks, Ken — but don't let us keep you any longer."

Ken Sharp arose. "Sure, Brian. As a matter of fact, I was just — "

Casey reached out a hand and touched his sleeve. "No. Don't go, Ken. Stay and have lunch with us."

Brian spoke up quickly. "Let him go, Casey. I'm *sure* he has an important business lunch he has to get to."

Sharp snapped his fingers. "Right! Thanks for reminding me, pal!" He winked at Casey.

"See you around, Casey."

Casey waited only long enough for Ken Sharp to be out of earshot. "What was *that* all about?" she asked angrily.

"I decided just now I don't like him. He's a creep," Brian replied calmly.

Casey shoved her chair back and jumped up. "For your information, that 'creep' just had some nice things to say about you."

Brian shook his head. "And I *still* say he's a creep!"

"And *I* say, you're no gentleman!" Casey stomped off. Brian made no move to stop her; the lunch with Casey that he'd looked forward to was ruined, anyway.

Brian was still in a dismal mood all the next morning. He went down to his workshop, Rascal trotting after him. "Can you believe it?" he asked Rascal. "This is the day of the big test— the most important day of my life—and Casey and I have had an argument." He lifted Chomps to the worktable and opened the side panel. "How am I supposed to concentrate on my work?"

Rascal looked on with interest as Brian began to make a few delicate adjustments in Chomps' many mechanisms. "All I said,"

Brian went on, "was that Ken Sharp is a creep."

Rascal stretched out on the floor, nose on paws, and began to look bored by this topic. Brian turned to Chomps. "Well, you check out okay. Except for that mystery malfunction of taking off without a signal, *you*, at least, don't give me any trouble at all."

He closed the panel. "Mmm. Maybe I could whip up an electronic Casey. That might solve all the problems." He lifted Chomps into the carrying case. "Just for safekeeping, I'll put you on 'watchdog.' Twenty-one, Chomps!"

Chomps' eyes began to glow at the command signal, and closing the carrier, Brian went up the stairs from the workshop, Rascal following. He put the carrier down near Rascal's own doggy-door.

Still muttering to himself, he left the house. "For all I know, Casey's having lunch with that creep right now!"

So far, Rascal had found the day rather dull. He watched Brian out of sight. Then, as he'd often done before, he departed by way of his doggie door for Monster's yard.

But this time there was no Casey to defend him when he came scooting for home, Monster

roaring behind him. He made it up the driveway and in the nick of time dived through his
own private entrance.

Monster was not giving up. He sped up the
drive looking as though he'd come crashing
right on in.

Hastily, Rascal glanced in Chomps' direction. He moved his paw toward the carrier
latch. FLIP. The door swung open and
Chomps trotted out. At the same time, Monster shoved his frightening head through the
doggie door. His raging bark stopped at mid-
note. *Two* Rascals!

The sight was too much for his nerves.
Pulling back he managed to get his head out-
doors to join the rest of him.

The bookend look-alikes each stared after
him. Then Chomps, eyes glowing, made his
move. Out he tore, down the driveway after
the intruder.

Rascal watched for a moment. Seeing
Chomps had the situation under control, he sat
down calmly and yawned. He yawned again
and glanced at Chomps' comfortable carrier.
With one last relaxing stretch of his furry
frame, he stepped into the little shelter. Ar-
ranging himself in a circle, he settled down for
a quiet, early afternoon snooze.

While Chomps was running the unhappy Monster halfway across Hamilton, Brian came home. Rascal scarcely bothered to open an eye and Brian certainly didn't bother to check the carrier. Minutes later the front doorbell rang. R.J. Norton stood there, the picture of happiness.

"What a day, Foster! What a day for the demonstration!" R.J. exclaimed. "After today, the sky's the limit!" He stepped into the house. "I gave the whole office the day off to celebrate!"

Brian closed the door. "That's terrific, Mr. Norton," he said gloomily.

R.J. looked at him sharply. "What's the matter, Foster?" His eyes suddenly widened. "It's Chomps!" he exclaimed fearfully. "He's malfunctioned again? You've lost him"? He's short-circuited?"

Brian sighed. "No. It's Casey."

"*Casey* short-circuited?"

"Did she ever! We had a misunderstanding, sir."

Norton sighed in relief. "Oh. Just that? Probably nothing. She never mentioned it to me."

"We had a stupid argument yesterday." Brian explained. He pulled on his jacket. "And

I've got to talk to her right now."

"*Now!*" R. J. couldn't believe his ears. "But, Foster — the demonstration!"

"I've got to see Casey first," said Brian. He ran out past his boss, and hopped into his car.

R.J. called angrily from the front door. "Foster, this demonstration is more important!"

"Not to me, it isn't," Brian, already backing his car down the driveway, called back over his shoulder. "I'll be right back."

R.J. looked around furiously. Not seeing the dog carrier in the room, he strode toward the kitchen. "Well, *I'm* not waiting," he muttered. "If he thinks I'm going to sit here and twiddle my thumbs while a multi-million dollar contract goes down the drain — well, he's very much mistaken!"

Rascal, still asleep, was startled to feel himself being joggled upward and to note the carrier door was closed. In no time at all he was being whisked to the football field in R.J.'s Cadillac.

In Gibbs' office Ken Sharp reported his latest "news," and Carl Gibbs was not at all pleased. "The football field! What kind of demonstration? No. Never mind. I'll find out for myself. I'll *be* there."

"This could work *for* us, Mr. Gibbs," Ken Sharp said hurriedly.

"Like how?"

Sharp smiled. "I hadn't come to the good part. Norton has given the entire staff the day off. Plans for Chomps are in his safe. So—"

"I get it!" Gibbs exclaimed. "Who needs the *dog* if I've got the plans?"

"Right!"

Gibbs chuckled. "Good thinking, Sharp. And with Norton at the demonstration and his office closed, getting the plans should be a snap—even for those two clowns you've had working for you."

Sharp nodded. "I'll take care of it. Depend on it."

During this time that Rascal was on his way to the football field and Ken Sharp was tattling all he knew to the head of Gibbs Guardian, Chomps had been far from idle.

An exhausted Monster panted into his own backyard and dived into the protection of his doghouse. Protection? Chomps was on it like a tiger. Monster's shelter was shaken in

Chomps' jaws as though it were an old slipper. Walls and roof began flying apart.

Finally, when Chomps called it a day, all that was left was the stunned Monster, lying flat and miserable under his wrecked residence. Miserably, he put his paws over his eyes and peeked out fearfully as Chomps trotted off for home.

True to his word, Brian came back as he'd promised R.J. But this time, Casey was in the passenger seat.

"That was all such a silly misunderstanding, Casey," Brian said for the fourth time. He stopped the car in the driveway.

"You're right," Casey agreed. "I didn't mean half the things I said."

"What about the other half?" Brian asked.

Casey threw her arms around him. "This is the other half." She kissed him.

Almost in the middle of this pleasant event, Brian's eyes flew open. "Hey! Your Dad's car isn't here!"

"I thought you said he was waiting to go to the demonstration."

Brian frowned. "He must have gone on ahead." He got out of the car. "I'll go in and get Chomps."

Sailing over Mrs. Fowler's hedge and landing right in front of Brian came the triumphant Chomps, fresh from his victory over Monster. His eyes glowed.

"Chomps!" Brian exclaimed. "Chomps! Twelve!"

Chomps lost the glow in his eyes. And Brian almost lost the glow in his. "Casey! Your father took Rascal!"

"Oh, Brian! No!"

Brian rushed in—and out—of the house. "The carrier's gone, all right. I don't know how Rascal got in it. I left the door closed." He clapped his hand to his head and groaned. "With Rascal he could blow the whole demonstration!"

"Well, don't *stand* there!" Casey exclaimed. "We've got to stop him!"

10

Lined up along the goal line of the football field stood six half-tracks. At the far end of the field a group of spectators stood on a raised platform near the entrance.

In this group, R.J. talked with the five engineers representing York Systems. At his feet was the C.H.O.M.P.S. carrier with Rascal peering out at the unusual view. He had never seen an electronic control system. As for the six driverless half-tracks, the noise of their big motors idling was something new to Rascal's ears. And he'd never seen anything that looked like a regular four-wheeled truck in front and something like a military tank at the other end with caterpillar tracks.

York's first engineer operated the control system. "All vehicles in place and ready," he called out.

The head engineer nodded. "All right, Mr. Norton. Here's the test York Systems has set up for your Canine Home Protection System. See those six rectangles we've set up at the end of the field? Now along the yard lines electronic circles show where we've placed buried land mines — one in the path of each of our six half...tracks."

R.J. nodded. "I understand," he said. "But what do you want my new security system to do?"

"We're interested in the electronic dog's ability to detect the hidden explosives." He pointed to the control board. "Only *one* of the mines is live. We'd expect your system to detect which one."

"The Norton Industries Canine Home Protection System can do that and anything else you and your engineers can dream up," R.J. said cheerfully.

"Very well. We'll proceed. On signal, the vehicles will start rolling down our 'obstacle' course." He nodded to the first engineer.

As his assistant pressed a series of buttons,

R.J. kneeled down and opened the carrier. "Okay, Chomps. Twenty-one!"

"All systems 'go,'" called the head engineer.

Rascal wasn't at all anxious to enter the big, unknown world outside the carrier. He backed up a trifle.

R.J.'s face flushed and the engineers exchanged glances.

"Come on, boy," R.J. coaxed. "This is your big chance." He looked up at the Head Engineer. "Maybe I have the signal wrong. I *thought* he was programmed for 'twenty-one.'" He turned back to Rascal. "Twenty-two? Twenty-three? Four? Fourteen?"

Rascal stretched, then stepped out of the carrier. He thumped his tail once, stood up, and gave R.J. a friendly kiss.

"Good boy, Chomps!" R.J. was delighted. He looked over at the York engineers. "Watch him, he's a killer."

The "killer" wagged his tail furiously and barked a happy greeting to one and all.

"That's — er — all part of his deceptive appearance," R.J. explained, looking rather foolish.

"He could fool *me*!" exclaimed the second engineer.

Norton put a hand on either side of Rascal's

head and turned it toward the football field. "Okay, Chomps. Now — *go* out and *get that mine!*" He pointed to center field. "Go on, boy, go on!"

A game! Rascal was all for it. He jumped down from the platform and raced toward the moving half-tracks. He barked joyously, nimbly scampering from one to another, and even nipping bravely at the big tires.

The engineers looked from Rascal's unbusinesslike antics to the President of Norton Industries. "If he works on numbers," said he head engineer, "he's not computing."

Norton's faith in Chomps remained. "He has plenty of time to find the live mine yet. He probably got a fix on it as soon as he hit the field."

The half-tracks were now at the thirty-yard line. Rascal still scampered playfully about in the big new playground. From one of the field buildings, Carl Gibbs watched all this through binoculars. "If that's a demonstration, I won't have to *buy* Norton out — he'll *give* me the business."

York Systems' head engineer frowned. "This wouldn't be some sort of a... well, practical joke, would it?"

R.J. was shocked. "Gentlemen! You've got

to remember that you're looking at a revolutionary new concept in security systems. What you're seeing might *look* strange — "

"It does," the head engineer said. The others nodded in agreement.

R.J. shook his head. "I must point out that Chomps has passed over the first four of the dummy mines without the slightest hesitation."

"Agreed," said the York head engineer. "But I have to wonder if it's because he hasn't the *slightest* idea of what he's doing."

"Impossible!" R.J. exclaimed. "You forget — you're not looking at a *real* dog, but a complicated, dynamic, computerized system."

"He's dynamic, all right," one of the York men laughed as Rascal frisked gaily in and out between the big machines.

R.J. was firm. "He's got another twenty yards to go. I promise you. He'll be zeroing in on that explosive any second now."

But as he spoke those confident words, a terrible idea came to him. If Chomps were malfunctioning, there's be no chance for Brian to make a repair. R.J. paled. "My only model of the new security systems will blow sky-high!" But before he could turn paler, Chomps' inventor brought his car to a screeching stop at the entrance by the platform. He, Casey, and Chomps leaped out and came forward at a gallop.

"Mr. Norton! Mr. Norton!"

"Dad! Dad!"

"Foster! Casey! Glad you made it. Chomps is zeroing in on the land mine."

It was Brian who turned pale. "*Land mine!*"

"Right," R.J. smiled. "He's programmed on 'watchdog,' so neutralizing a live mine should be a cinch."

Casey didn't wait for Brian's reply. She ran out on the field at top speed. "Rascal! Rascal! *Stop!*"

"*Rascal!*" R.J. nearly fainted.

Brian paid no attention to his future father-in-law's state of health. "Chomps! Twenty-one! *Go*, Chomps!"

Chomps spun around, stared across the field, and took off, eyes blazing. His X-ray vision instantly revealed the buried land mine on the ten-yard line. And Rascal was frolicking dangerously close! At top speed he flashed ahead.

"*Two* of them!" the entire group of engineers exclaimed.

"What's going on?" asked the head engineer. "Norton — what's this all about?"

"The trucks!" Norton yelled. "Stop those trucks! That's a *real* dog out there!"

The first engineer pushed the control button. Nothing happened. Frantically he pushed it again. "It's not responding!" he yelled desperately.

And Rascal, a scant three feet from the fatal ten-yard line, was given a shoulder bump from Chomps that sent him yelping to one side.

Moving on past, Chomps made one of his skidding stops. Frantically, he began to dig as the huge wheels of the sixth half-track rolled closer and closer.

Chomps ducked his head down into the hole he'd engineered. Immediately, he backed out, the land mine clamped in his jaws. Giving a fast spin, he zipped away just as the death-dealing wheels passed over the hole.

From the outbuilding, Gibbs dropped his binoculars. *"Two* of them?" He backed away from the entrance of the building. And racing for the same entrance came Chomps. In he dove, spun around, made a wild exit from the entrance, and *sat down*.

Everyone on the platform held their breaths, covered their ears, and froze.

A moment later the expected deafening explosion came. The building burst apart in a cloud of smoke and debris. A tattered figure, looking like a coal-miner, slowly emerged from the ruins, shaking and muttering.

Chomps scarcely moved. When Brian, Norton, Casey, and Rascal came rushing to him, his blazing eyes never turned from the smoking wreck.

"*Terrific*, Chomps!"

"You're a hero, Chomps!"

"You saved Rascal's life."

"Fantastic, Chomps! What a performance!"

Rascal added a grateful bark to that chorus.

But their compliments came to a sudden end as the President of Gibbs Guardian, clothes in smoking tatters, came reeling toward them. "That dog is a menace!" he yelled chokingly.

R.J. spun to look at the owner of the voice. "Gibbs! What are *you* doing here?"

Gibbs looked down at his tattered outfit. "I'm asking myself that same question right now!"

R.J. turned a deep, angry red. "You were spying! Admit it! You were spying!"

The York engineering group having successfully stopped the half-tracks, looked and listened. "Let them worry about whatever they're worrying about," the head engineer muttered. "Come on, boys. Let's go. We've a real report to send the home office! Never saw anything like it."

Gibbs was leaving, too; he tottered in the direction of his car. R.J., Casey, Brian, Rascal, and the new successful security system followed right behind him. "What if I was spying?" Gibbs bellowed. "You're a competitor. And I make it my business to know what my competitors are doing."

"But you admit to spying!" Norton exclaimed, raging.

The group reached the place where Gibbs' car was parked.

"You don't know it yet but you're almost out of business, Norton," Gibbs snarled.

"What's he talking about, Mr. Norton?" Brian asked.

"What do you mean 'out of business'? Didn't you see that fantastic demonstration?" Casey glared.

"I think you'd better explain yourself, Gibbs," R.J. demanded.

Gibbs moved straight to his car, opening the door. "I don't have to explain *anything* to you, Norton."

Hardly had he finished speaking than a voice came crackling over the car's CB radio, "Pussycat to Fat Cat. Over. Contacted my men and they're on their way to Norton's."

Gibbs suddenly looked as though he'd bit into a very sour lemon as the voice continued. "'Operation Plans' is a cinch. Over."

Casey was first to put it all together. "Dad! They're breaking into your office to get the plans for Chomps! And Mr. Gibbs — you're 'Fat Cat,' aren't you?"

"Over? Hello? Over? Hello? Pussycat to Fat Cat," Ken Sharp's crackled-up voice asked.

Brian frowned. "Who's voice is that? Who's Pussycat?"

Casey grabbed his hand. "Who cares right now? We've got to get over there and stop them!"

Off they went, followed by Rascal and Chomps. Norton stayed behind long enough to glare at Gibbs and exclaim scornfully, "*Fat* cat, eh! Skinny cat, Gibbs! And very soon."

11

Norton Industries' parking lot was empty except for Ken Sharp's car and the van driven by Brooks and Bracken. The three met at the locked front door of the building.

Bracken slowly read the sign hung inside the door, "CLOSED FOR C.H.O.M.P.S.' DAY." Ken Sharp unlocked the door and the three hurried in.

Sharp pointed to the staircase. "Now, listen! The plans are in Norton's safe on the third floor. I'll disconnect the alarm system so you can get inside the office—but I'll have to reset it, so the disconnect won't register."

"Got it," Brooks said. He patted the black bag he carried. "No problem."

"So when you get the plans," Sharp said hurriedly, "knock twice and I'll disconnect again. Got that? Knock *loud*."

"You can count on us," Brooks nodded.

"Just make it *fast*."

Brooks and Bracken started up the stairs. Ken Sharp moved to a wall panel. Opening it, he switched the alarm to OFF.

Up on the third floor, Brooks had no trouble picking the office door lock—the problem was going to be locating R.J.'s wall safe.

"Sharp said the safe was behind the desk," Bracken said, staring at the wall.

"I know *that*."

"Get started running your fingers on the paneling." Brooks slid his hands up and down. "Here it is!"

"Easy!" Bracken grinned.

Pressing the button, the panel instantly slid back. A good-sized safe stood on floor level. Brooks took out a stethoscope and began turning the dial.

"How's it comin', *Doc*?" Bracken snickered.

In the lobby Sharp nervously looked at his watch. "They must be in the office by now," he muttered. "I'd better switch the alarm back to ON."

111

Upstairs Bracken repeated his question. As there was still no reply from his pal, he reached down and spoke into the dangling tube of the stethoscope. "How's it comin', Doc, I said." It was like a clap of thunder in Brooks' ears. He ripped off the stethoscope.

"Bracken!"

"Did I say something wrong?" Bracken asked innocently.

"Aw, forget it," Brooks said furiously. "We're just gonna have to blow this safe open."

He reached into his black bag and working with long wires quickly set a plastic explosive. "Here, Bracken," he said handing over a timing device. "Set the timer."

Bracken stared down. The timer looked like the face of a clock.

"Uh — Brooks. I forget. Is the big hand or the little hand the hour hand?"

Brooks fumed. He yanked back the timer. "Can't you do *anything*?" Shaking his head, he did the setting and placed it at the base of the safe.

TICK-TICK-TICK. Satisfied with the sound, Brooks stood up. "There. Now we got three minutes to get outta here before the safe goes."

They headed for the door. Bracken quickly reached for the doorknob. "Allow me," he said. politely. He turned the knob.

DING! DING! DING! Alarms went off all over the building. DING DING DING!

"Bracken! The signal! You were supposed to knock twice!"

"The police! They'll be here any minute! Come on. We gotta get outta here. We'll use the window."

"Okay," Bracken agreed. "Sorry about the knock. I mean, the two knocks."

"Will you *come on*," Brooks yelled.

They reached the window in time to see a car come roaring into the parking lot and pull to a stop at the front entrance.

"Not the police," said Bracken interestedly.

Brian, Casey, Rascal, and Chomps leaped out of the car. Brooks and Bracken groaned. "They got *two*!" Bracken almost cried.

"Let's just wait for the police!"

"Get *going*," Brooks grated. "Can't you hear that tick-ticking?"

"Well, no. Not with all this other noise."

"OUT!" Brooks roared, opening the window. "Reach for the rainspout, dummy!"

Ken Sharp, a nervous wreck, pushed out of

the lobby just as Brian, Casey, and Company pushed in.

"Sharp!" Brian exclaimed. "What are you doing in here?"

Sharp nearly babbled a reply. "I—uh, I just stopped by the office. The alarms went off. Somebody must be breaking in."

"Some of Gibbs' goons, I'll bet," said Casey.

Ken Sharp pushed past them. "I'm going to get the police," he quaked.

Brian stared at R.J.'s second-in-command. "Wait!" he suddenly yelled. *"You're* 'Pussycat!'"

Sharp raced to his car, jumped in, gunned the engine—and Brooks and Bracken dropped out of nowhere in time to drive off with him!

"Brian! We've got to stop them! Let's go!"

Brian caught her elbow. "We can't do it. But Chomps can! Chomps! Twenty-one!"

Chomps' eyes hardly had begun their glow before he was off and away after the fleeing car.

"Come on, Casey. Let's see if they got the plans." They ran inside the building.

TICK-TICK-TICK! And Casey and Brian were right outside R.J.'s office door!

★   ★   ★

Chomps passed Sharp's car with ease, and dashed ahead to a tall metal flagpole at the parking lot entry gate. He gave it his best "karate" chop.

"Brakes!" Sharp yelled. "Hang on!"

"Turn! *Turn!*" yelled Brooks.

Too late. The flagpole fell square in front of the front wheels. The car crashed against it and came to a steamy halt. Chomps' work was not done. He raced back to the rear of the car and seized the bumper. Shaking it wildly, he got the results he wanted.

Hood, trunk, fenders, wheels—all flew off. The doors shook open. And hard as Sharp, Brooks, and Bracken tried to hang on, out they flew, sprawling on the pavement. Unluckily, they sprawled right in front of a speeding police car. Brakes screeched. Officers stepped out.

Chomps didn't hang around to see what happened next. His ears perked up at the sound of the distant timer. Getting a fix on its location he raced back to the building. Flinging himself through the open door, he raced on to the third floor.

Brian and Casey were already heading for the safe. "The panel's open!" Casey cried.

"They found the safe."

"With Sharp's help no doubt," Brian said angrily. "Hey! Casey. Look! They've got an explosive on it."

For the first time they realized they were hearing a TICK-TICK. "Run, Casey!"

But they were nearly knocked flat as Chomps bounded past them. He grabbed the explosive in his jaws. There was no hesitation. Brian and Casey together couldn't have stopped him from the next horrendous act!

Taking a mighty leap, Chomps sailed out the open window.

"Oh, no!" Casey moaned.

They raced to the window. "Chomps!" Brian cried out desperately.

Mid-air it happened. An explosion lighted the sky like fireworks on the Fourth of July. "Chomps!" Casey screamed — and buried her head against Brian's chest. "Oh, Brian," she cried. "Don't look!"

"We'll go downstairs," Brian said dully. "There are the police — we'll have to explain."

On the parking lot, Sharp, Brook, and Bracken were locked in the police car. The officers stood staring up at the now smoky sky. "What *was* it, anyway?" asked the first officer.

But Brian and Casey could not bear to wait to explain. They rushed to the wreckage of Chomps. All his electronic wizardry was in the plain sight. Casey burst into tears. "Oh, Chomps," Brian gently put his hand on her shoulder. "Casey, he wasn't *real*. Remember that!"

But Rascal didn't seem to share Brian's view. He ran past them both and sniffed mournfully at the familiar scent of Chomps' small broken frame. He whimpered. Then suddenly as he'd come, he ran back to the car.

The police came over. "We got an alarm and we picked up those three. Can you give us any information on this?"

Before Brian could reply, Rascal was back — this time with the favorite toy he'd often tried to share with Chomps.

He put the small plastic bone in front of Chomps' sad muzzle and whimpered again.

Brian's eyes glimmered wetly. "I'm afraid it's too late, Rascal," he said gently.

"Brian! Look. Look at Chomps' eyes."

Slowly, slowly the old glow was coming back.

Brian stared. "His eyes? Casey, look at his *tail*!"

For the very first time, Chomps' tail was wagging. It wasn't much, but it *was* a wag.

Brian, Casey, and Rascal's spirits zoomed upward. "It *isn't* too late," Casey cried.

The police officer shook his head. "I don't get it. What's going on?"

12

Exactly one week had passed since the events of Demonstration Day. York Systems was happy. J.R. Norton was happier. And Brian, Casey, and Rascal were perhaps happiest of all. Gibbs and his goon squad, including Ken Sharp, were unhappy.

Casey sat on Brian's front steps, her arms around Rascal, as Brian talked with her father.

"When do you think we can go into production on the system, Brian?" R.J. asked.

"Within the month, I hope, sir." He turned toward the open front door. "Chomps! Fortynine!"

Out trotted a renewed Chomps. He stepped briskly over to Casey and Rascal. Casey patted his head. But Rascal scrambled from her arms and stared at the front door.

Out came two *more* Chomps. They promptly joined the growing group on the front steps.

R.J. nearly jumped for joy. "*Three* Chompses?"

Brian grinned. He nodded. "Hand-produced," he said. "Now we have extra models for testing."

"Brian, that's incredible!"

Brian looked pleased. "And I *think* I've licked the problem of malfunction. At least it hasn't shown up yet."

Next door Mrs. Fowler came out on her porch. "Brian," she called over. "Is Muffin with you?"

"Sorry, Mrs. Fowler. I haven't seen her," Brian called back.

"Oh, dear. Well, I'll just use my whistle. It usually works."

The whistle pitch was so high that it seemed impossible for Muffin to hear it. But out she trotted from the hedge. And at the same time the *three* Chompses leaped to their feet. Three pairs of eyes glowed red.

Suddenly the models for the Canine Home Protection System went careening off the steps and racing down the street, barking madly. Rascal turned his head first to one side, then the other. It seemed to help him decide on a course of action. Scrambling out of Casey's arms he took out after the C.H.O.M.P.S. team to join in whatever game might develop.

"Rascal!" Casey cried.

"What's happening?" R.J. asked, bewildered by this turn of events.

It was Brian who guessed right. Excitedly, he jumped to his feet. "That's it! That's the cause of the malfunction."

Casey and her father stared. "What's the cause?" Casey asked.

"Mrs. Fowler's dog whistle. It hits the computer programming circuitry. That's why it malfunctions!"

But for Monster, life was going from bad to worse. Padding over his lawn he saw FOUR identical "Rascals" come tearing along.

It was too much. Dropping down behind the potted ferns, he made himself as small as possible and covered his head with his big paws.

Luck was with him! The sounds of barking went right on and faded into the distance.

Monster stood up, breathed deeply, and glanced over at his wrecked doghouse.

Canine Home Protection System, indeed!